MY LADY GREENSLEEVES

ISBN 979-8-8809-0859-2

MY LADY GREENSLEEVES

by Frederik Pohl

This guard smelled trouble and it could be counted on to come—for a nose for trouble was one of the many talents bred here!

I

His name was Liam O'Leary and there was something stinking in his nostrils. It was the smell of trouble. He hadn't found what the trouble was yet, but he would. That was his business. He was a captain of guards in Estates-General Correctional Institution—better known to its inmates as the Jug—and if he hadn't been able to detect the scent of trouble brewing a cell-block away, he would never have survived to reach his captaincy.

And her name, he saw, was Sue-Ann Bradley, Detainee No. WFA-656R.

He frowned at the rap sheet, trying to figure out what got a girl like her into a place like this. And, what was more important, why she couldn't adjust herself to it, now that she was in.

He demanded: "Why wouldn't you mop out your cell?"

The girl lifted her head angrily and took a step forward. The block guard, Sodaro, growled warningly: "Watch it, auntie!"

O'Leary shook his head. "Let her talk, Sodaro." It said in the *Civil Service Guide to Prison Administration*: "Detainees will be permitted to speak in their own behalf in disciplinary proceedings." And O'Leary was a man who lived by the book.

She burst out: "I never got a chance! That old witch Mathias never told me I was supposed to mop up. She banged on the door and said, 'Slush up, sister!' And then, ten minutes later, she called the guards and told them I refused to mop."

The block guard guffawed. "Wipe talk—that's what she was telling you to do. Cap'n, you know what's funny about this? This Bradley is—"

"Shut up, Sodaro."

*

Captain O'leary put down his pencil and looked at the girl. She was attractive and young—not beyond hope, surely. Maybe she had got off to a wrong start, but the question was, would putting her in the disciplinary block help straighten her out? He rubbed his ear and looked past her at the line of prisoners on the rap detail, waiting for him to judge their cases.

5

MY LADY GREENSLEEVES

He said patiently: "Bradley, the rules are you have to mop out your cell. If you didn't understand what Mathias was talking about, you should have asked her. Now I'm warning you, the next time—"

"Hey, Cap'n, wait!" Sodaro was looking alarmed. "This isn't a first offense. Look at the rap sheet. Yesterday she pulled the same thing in the mess hall." He shook his head reprovingly at the prisoner. "The block guard had to break up a fight between her and another wench, and she claimed the same business—said she didn't understand when the other one asked her to move along." He added virtuously: "The guard warned her then that next time she'd get the Greensleeves for sure."

Inmate Bradley seemed to be on the verge of tears. She said tautly: "I don't care. I don't care!"

O'Leary stopped her. "That's enough! Three days in Block O!"

It was the only thing to do—for her own sake as much as for his. He had managed, by strength of will, not to hear that she had omitted to say "sir" every time she spoke to him, but he couldn't keep it up forever and he certainly couldn't overlook hysteria. And hysteria was clearly the next step for her.

All the same, he stared after her as she left. He handed the rap sheet to Sodaro and said absently: "Too bad a kid like her has to be here. What's she in for?"

"You didn't know, Cap'n?" Sodaro leered. "She's in for conspiracy to violate the Categoried Class laws. Don't waste your time with her, Cap'n. She's a figger-lover!"

Captain O'Leary took a long drink of water from the fountain marked "Civil Service." But it didn't wash the taste out of his mouth, the smell from his nose.

What got into a girl to get her mixed up with that kind of dirty business? He checked out of the cell blocks and walked across the yard, wondering about her. She'd had every advantage—decent Civil Service parents, a good education, everything a girl could wish for. If anything, she had had a better environment than O'Leary himself, and look what she had made of it.

The direction of evolution is toward specialization and Man is no exception, but with the difference that his is the one species that creates its own environment in which to specialize. From the moment that clans formed, specialization began—the hunters using the weapons made by the flint-chippers, the food cooked in clay pots made by the ceramists, over fire made by the shaman who guarded the sacred flame.

Civilization merely increased the extent of specialization. From the born mechanic and the man with the gift of gab, society evolved to the point of smaller contact and less communication between the specializations, until now they could understand each other on only the most basic physical necessities—and not even always then.

But this was desirable, for the more specialists, the higher the degree of civilization. The ultimate should be the complete segregation of each specialization—social and genetic measures to make them breed true, because the unspecialized man is an uncivilized man, or at any rate he does not advance civilization. And letting the specializations mix would produce genetic undesirables: clerk-laborer or Professional-GI misfits, for example, being only half specialized, would be good at no specialization.

And the basis of this specialization society was: "The aptitude groups are the true races of mankind." Putting it into law was only the legal enforcement of a demonstrable fact.

"Evening, Cap'n." A bleary old inmate orderly stood up straight and touched his cap as O'Leary passed by.

"Evening."

*

O'Leary noted, with the part of his mind that always noted those things, that the orderly had been leaning on his broom until he'd noticed the captain coming by. Of course, there wasn't much to sweep—the spray machines and sweeperdozers had been over the cobblestones of the yard twice already that day. But it was an inmate's job to keep busy. And it was a guard captain's job to notice when they didn't.

There wasn't anything wrong with that job, he told himself. It was a perfectly good civil-service position—better than post-office clerk, not as good as Congressman, but a job you could be proud to hold. He *was* proud of it. It was *right* that he should be proud of it. He was civil-service born and bred, and naturally he was proud and content to do a good, clean civil-service job.

If he had happened to be born a fig—a *clerk*, he corrected himself—if he had happened to be born a clerk, why, he would have been proud of that, too. There wasn't anything wrong with being a clerk—or a mechanic or a soldier, or even a laborer, for that matter.

Good laborers were the salt of the Earth! They weren't smart, maybe, but they had a—well, a sort of natural, relaxed joy of living. O'Leary was a broad-minded man and many times he had thought almost with a touch of envy how *comfortable* it must be to be a wipe—a *laborer*. No responsibilities. No worries. Just an easy, slow routine of work and loaf, work and loaf.

Of course, he wouldn't *really* want that kind of life, because he was Civil Service and not the kind to try to cross over class barriers that weren't *meant* to be—

"Evening, Cap'n."

He nodded to the mechanic inmate who was, theoretically, in charge of maintaining the prison's car pool, just inside the gate.

"Evening, Conan," he said.

Conan, now—he was a big buck greaser and he would be there for the next hour, languidly poking a piece of fluff out of the air filter on the prison jeep. Lazy, sure. Undependable, certainly. But he kept the cars going—and, O'Leary thought approvingly, when his sentence was up in another year or so, he would go back to his life with his status restored, a mechanic on the outside as he had been inside, and he certainly would never risk coming back to the Jug by trying to pass as Civil Service or anything else. He knew his place.

So why didn't this girl, this Sue-Ann Bradley, know hers?

II

Every prison has its Greensleeves—sometimes they are called by different names. Old Marquette called it "the canary;" Louisiana State called it "the red hats;" elsewhere it was called "the hole," "the snake pit," "the Klondike." When you're in it, you don't much care what it is called; it is a place for punishment.

And punishment is what you get.

Block O in Estates-General Correctional Institution was the disciplinary block, and because of the green straitjackets its inhabitants wore, it was called the Greensleeves. It was a community of its own, an enclave within the larger city-state that was the Jug. And like any other community, it had its leading citizens ... two of them. Their names were Sauer and Flock.

8

Sue-Ann Bradley heard them before she reached the Greensleeves. She was in a detachment of three unfortunates like herself, convoyed by an irritable guard, climbing the steel steps toward Block O from the floor below, when she heard the yelling.

"Owoo-o-o," screamed Sauer from one end of the cell block and "Yow-w-w!" shrieked Flock at the other.

The inside deck guard of Block O looked nervously at the outside deck guard. The outside guard looked impassively back—after all, he was on the outside.

The inside guard muttered: "Wipe rats! They're getting on my nerves."

The outside guard shrugged.

"Detail, *halt*!" The two guards turned to see what was coming in as the three new candidates for the Greensleeves slumped to a stop at the head of the stairs. "Here they are," Sodaro told them. "Take good care of 'em, will you? Especially the lady—she's going to like it here, because there's plenty of wipes and greasers and figgers to keep her company." He laughed coarsely and abandoned his charges to the Block O guards.

The outside guard said sourly: "A woman, for God's sake. Now O'Leary knows I hate it when there's a woman in here. It gets the others all riled up."

"Let them in," the inside guard told him. "The others are riled up already."

Sue-Ann Bradley looked carefully at the floor and paid them no attention. The outside guard pulled the switch that turned on the tanglefoot electronic fields that swamped the floor of the block corridor and of each individual cell. While the fields were on, you could ignore the prisoners—they simply could not move fast enough, against the electronic drag of the field, to do any harm. But it was a rule that, even in Block O, you didn't leave the tangler fields on all the time—only when the cell doors had to be opened or a prisoner's restraining garment removed.

Sue-Ann walked bravely forward through the opened gate—and fell flat on her face. It was her first experience of a tanglefoot field. It was like walking through molasses.

The guard guffawed and lifted her up by one shoulder. "Take it easy, auntie. Come on, get in your cell." He steered her in the right direction and pointed to a greensleeved straitjacket on the cell cot. "Put that on.

9

Being as you're a lady, we won't tie it up, but the rules say you got to wear it and the rules—Hey. She's crying!" He shook his head, marveling. It was the first time he had ever seen a prisoner cry in the Greensleeves.

However, he was wrong. Sue-Ann's shoulders were shaking, but not from tears. Sue-Ann Bradley had got a good look at Sauer and at Flock as she passed them by and she was fighting off an almost uncontrollable urge to retch.

*

Sauer and Flock were what are called prison wolves. They were laborers—"wipes," for short—or, at any rate, they had been once. They had spent so much time in prisons that it was sometimes hard even for them to remember what they really were, outside. Sauer was a big, grinning redhead with eyes like a water moccasin. Flock was a lithe five-footer with the build of a water moccasin—and the sad, stupid eyes of a calf.

Sauer stopped yelling for a moment. "Hey, Flock!"

"What do you want, Sauer?" called Flock from his own cell.

"We got a lady with us! Maybe we ought to cut out this yelling so as not to disturb the lady!" He screeched with howling, maniacal laughter. "Anyway, if we don't cut this out, they'll get us in trouble, Flock!"

"Oh, you think so?" shrieked Flock. "Jeez, I wish you hadn't said that, Sauer. You got me scared! I'm so scared, I'm gonna have to yell!"

The howling started all over again.

The inside guard finished putting the new prisoners away and turned off the tangler field once more. He licked his lips. "Say, you want to take a turn in here for a while?"

"Uh-uh." The outside guard shook his head.

"You're yellow," the inside guard said moodily. "Ah, I don't know why I don't quit this lousy job. Hey, you! Pipe down or I'll come in and beat your head off!"

"Ee-ee-ee!" screamed Sauer in a shrill falsetto. "I'm scared!" Then he grinned at the guard, all but his water-moccasin eyes. "Don't you know you can't hurt a wipe by hitting him on the head, Boss?"

"Shut *up*!" yelled the inside guard.

Sue-Ann Bradley's weeping now was genuine. She simply could not help it. The crazy yowling of the hard-timers, Sauer and Flock, was getting under her skin. They weren't even—even *human*, she told herself

10

miserably, trying to weep silently so as not to give the guards the satisfaction of hearing her—they were animals!

Resentment and anger, she could understand. She told herself doggedly that resentment and anger were natural and right. They were perfectly normal expressions of the freedom-loving citizen's rebellion against the vile and stifling system of Categoried Classes. It was *good* that Sauer and Flock still had enough spirit to struggle against the vicious system—

But did they have to scream so?

The senseless yelling was driving her crazy. She abandoned herself to weeping and she didn't even care who heard her any more. Senseless!

It never occurred to Sue-Ann Bradley that it might not be senseless, because noise hides noise. But then she hadn't been a prisoner very long.

III

"I smell trouble," said O'Leary to the warden.

"Trouble? Trouble?" Warden Schluckebier clutched his throat and his little round eyes looked terrified—as perhaps they should have. Warden Godfrey Schluckebier was the almighty Caesar of ten thousand inmates in the Jug, but privately he was a fussy old man trying to hold onto the last decent job he would have in his life.

"Trouble? *What* trouble?"

O'Leary shrugged. "Different things. You know Lafon, from Block A? This afternoon, he was playing ball with the laundry orderlies in the yard."

The warden, faintly relieved, faintly annoyed, scolded: "O'Leary, what did you want to worry me for? There's nothing wrong with playing ball in the yard. That's what recreation periods are for."

"You don't see what I mean, Warden. Lafon was a professional on the outside—an architect. Those laundry cons were laborers. Pros and wipes don't mix; it isn't natural. And there are other things."

O'Leary hesitated, frowning. How could you explain to the warden that it didn't *smell* right?

"For instance—Well, there's Aunt Mathias in the women's block. She's a pretty good old girl—that's why she's the block orderly. She's a lifer, she's got no place to go, she gets along with the other women. But today she put a woman named Bradley on report. Why? Because she told Bradley

11

to mop up in wipe talk and Bradley didn't understand. Now Mathias wouldn't—"

The warden raised his hand. "Please, O'Leary, don't bother me about that kind of stuff." He sighed heavily and rubbed his eyes. He poured himself a cup of steaming black coffee from a brewpot, reached in a desk drawer for something, hesitated, glanced at O'Leary, then dropped a pale blue tablet into the cup. He drank it down eagerly, ignoring the scalding heat.

He leaned back, looking suddenly happier and much more assured.

"O'Leary, you're a guard captain, right? And I'm your warden. You have your job, keeping the inmates in line, and I have mine. Now your job is just as important as my job," he said piously. "*Everybody's* job is just as important as everybody else's, right? But we have to stick to our own jobs. We don't want to try to *pass*."

O'Leary snapped erect, abruptly angry. Pass! What the devil way was that for the warden to talk to him?

"Excuse the expression, O'Leary," the warden said anxiously. "I mean, after all, 'Specialization is the goal of civilization,' right?" He was a great man for platitudes, was Warden Schluckebier. "*You* know you don't want to worry about *my* end of running the prison. And *I* don't want to worry about *yours*. You see?" And he folded his hands and smiled like a civil-service Buddha.

*

O'Leary choked back his temper. "Warden, I'm telling you that there's trouble coming up. I smell the signs."

"Handle it, then!" snapped the warden, irritated at last.

"But suppose it's too big to handle. Suppose—"

"It isn't," the warden said positively. "Don't borrow trouble with all your supposing, O'Leary." He sipped the remains of his coffee, made a wry face, poured a fresh cup and, with an elaborate show of not noticing what he was doing, dropped three of the pale blue tablets into it this time.

He sat beaming into space, waiting for the jolt to take effect.

"Well, then," he said at last. "You just remember what I've told you tonight, O'Leary, and we'll get along fine. 'Specialization is the—' Oh, curse the thing."

His phone was ringing. The warden picked it up irritably.

12

That was the trouble with those pale blue tablets, thought O'Leary; they gave you a lift, but they put you on edge.

"Hello," barked the warden, not even glancing at the viewscreen. "What the devil do you want? Don't you know I'm—What? You did *what*? You're going to WHAT?"

He looked at the viewscreen at last with a look of pure horror. Whatever he saw on it, it did not reassure him. His eyes opened like clamshells in a steamer.

"O'Leary," he said faintly, "my mistake."

And he hung up—more or less by accident; the handset dropped from his fingers.

The person on the other end of the phone was calling from Cell Block O.

Five minutes before, he hadn't been anywhere near the phone and it didn't look as if his chances of ever getting near it were very good. Because five minutes before, he was in his cell, with the rest of the hard-timers of the Greensleeves.

His name was Flock.

He was still yelling. Sue-Ann Bradley, in the cell across from him, thought that maybe, after all, the man was really in pain. Maybe the crazy screams were screams of agony, because certainly his face was the face of an agonized man.

The outside guard bellowed: "Okay, okay. Take ten!"

Sue-Ann froze, waiting to see what would happen. What actually did happen was that the guard reached up and closed the switch that actuated the tangler fields on the floors of the cells. The prison rules were humanitarian, even for the dregs that inhabited the Greensleeves. Ten minutes out of every two hours, even the worst case had to be allowed to take his hands out of the restraining garment.

"Rest period" it was called—in the rule book. The inmates had a less lovely term for it.

*

At the guard's yell, the inmates jumped to their feet.

Bradley was a little slow getting off the edge of the steel-slat bed—nobody had warned her that the eddy currents in the tangler fields had a way of making metal smoke-hot. She gasped but didn't cry out. Score one more painful lesson in her new language course. She rubbed the backs of her thighs gingerly—and slowly, slowly, for the eddy currents did not permit you to move fast. It was like pushing against rubber; the faster you tried to move, the greater the resistance.

The guard peered genially into her cell. "You're okay, auntie." She proudly ignored him as he slogged deliberately away on his rounds. He didn't have to untie her and practically stand over her while she attended to various personal matters, as he did with the male prisoners. It was not much to be grateful for, but Sue-Ann Bradley was grateful. At least she didn't have to live *quite* like a fig—like an underprivileged clerk, she told herself, conscience-stricken.

Across the hall, the guard was saying irritably: "What the hell's the matter with you?" He opened the door of the cell with an asbestos-handled key held in a canvas glove.

Flock was in that cell and he was doubled over.

The guard looked at him doubtfully. It could be a trick, maybe. Couldn't it? But he could see Flock's face and the agony in it was real enough. And Flock was gasping, through real tears: "Cramps. I—I—"

"Ah, you wipes always got a pain in the gut." The guard lumbered around Flock to the draw-strings at the back of the jacket. Funny smell in here, he told himself—not for the first time. And imagine, some people didn't believe that wipes had a smell of their own! But this time, he realized cloudily, it was a rather unusual smell. Something burning. Almost like meat scorching.

It wasn't pleasant. He finished untying Flock and turned away; let the stinking wipe take care of his own troubles. He only had ten minutes to get all the way around Block O and the inmates complained like crazy if he didn't make sure they all got the most possible free time. He was pretty good at snowshoeing through the tangler field. He was a little vain about it, even; at times he had been known to boast of his ability to make the rounds in two minutes, every time.

Every time but this.

For Flock moaned behind him, oddly close.

The guard turned, but not quickly enough. There was Flock—astonishingly, he was half out of his jacket; his arms hadn't been in

14

the sleeves at all! And in one of the hands, incredibly, there was something that glinted and smoked.

"All right," croaked Flock, tears trickling out of eyes nearly shut with pain.

But it wasn't the tears that held the guard; it was the shining, smoking thing, now poised at his throat. A shiv! It looked as though it had been made out of a bed-spring, ripped loose from its frame God knows how, hidden inside the greensleeved jacket God knows how—filed, filed to sharpness over endless hours.

No wonder Flock moaned—the eddy currents in the shiv were slowly cooking his hand; and the blister against his abdomen, where the shiv had been hidden during other rest periods, felt like raw acid.

*

"All right," whispered Flock, "just walk out the door and you won't get hurt. Unless the other screw makes trouble, you won't get hurt, so tell him not to, you hear?"

He was nearly fainting with the pain.

But he hadn't let go.

He didn't let go. And he didn't stop.

IV

It was Flock on the phone to the warden—Flock with his eyes still streaming tears, Flock with Sauer standing right behind him, menacing the two bound deck guards.

Sauer shoved Flock out of the way. "Hey, Warden!" he said, and the voice was a cheerful bray, though the serpent eyes were cold and hating. "Warden, you got to get a medic in here. My boy Flock, he hurt himself real bad and he needs a doctor." He gestured playfully at the guards with the shiv. "I tell you, Warden. I got this knife and I got your guards here. Enough said? So get a medic in here quick, you hear?"

And he snapped the connection.

O'Leary said: "Warden, I told you I smelled trouble!"

The warden lifted his head, glared, started feebly to speak, hesitated, and picked up the long-distance phone. He said sadly to the prison operator: "Get me the governor—fast."

MY LADY GREENSLEEVES

Riot!

The word spread out from the prison on seven-league boots.

It snatched the city governor out of a friendly game of Seniority with his manager and their wives—and just when he was holding the Porkbarrel Joker concealed in the hole.

It broke up the Base Championship Scramble Finals at Hap Arnold Field to the south, as half the contestants had to scramble in earnest to a Red Alert that was real.

It reached to police precinct houses and TV newsrooms and highway checkpoints, and from there it filtered into the homes and lives of the nineteen million persons that lived within a few dozen miles of the Jug.

Riot. And yet fewer than half a dozen men were involved.

A handful of men, and the enormous bulk of the city-state quivered in every limb and class. In its ten million homes, in its hundreds of thousands of public places, the city-state's people shook under the impact of the news from the prison.

For the news touched them where their fears lay. Riot! And not merely a street brawl among roistering wipes, or a bar-room fight of greasers relaxing from a hard day at the plant. The riot was down among the corrupt sludge that underlay the state itself. Wipes brawled with wipes and no one cared; but in the Jug, all classes were cast together.

*

Forty miles to the south, Hap Arnold Field was a blaze of light. The airmen tumbled out of their quarters and dayrooms at the screech of the alert siren, and behind them their wives and children stretched and yawned and worried. An alert! The older kids fussed and complained and their mothers shut them up. No, there wasn't any alert scheduled for tonight; no, they didn't know where Daddy was going; no, the kids couldn't get up yet—it was the middle of the night.

And as soon as they had the kids back in bed, most of the mothers struggled into their own airwac uniforms and headed for the briefing area to hear.

They caught the words from a distance—not quite correctly. "Riot!" gasped an aircraftswoman first-class, mother of three. "The wipes! I *told* Charlie they'd get out of hand and—Alys, we aren't safe. You know how

16

they are about GI women! I'm going right home and get a club and stand right by the door and—"

"Club!" snapped Alys, radarscope-sergeant, with two children querulously awake in her nursery at home. "What in God's name is the use of a club? You can't hurt a wipe by hitting him on the head. You'd better come along to Supply with me and draw a gun—you'll need it before this night is over."

But the airmen themselves heard the briefing loud and clear over the scramble-call speakers, and they knew it was not merely a matter of trouble in the wipe quarters. The Jug! The governor himself had called them out; they were to fly interdicting missions at such-and-such levels on such-and-such flight circuits around the prison.

The rockets took off on fountains of fire; and the jets took off with a whistling roar; and last of all, the helicopters took off ... and they were the ones who might actually accomplish something. They took up their picket posts on the prison perimeter, a pilot and two bombardiers in each 'copter, stone-faced, staring grimly alert at the prison below.

They were ready for the breakout.

But there wasn't any breakout.

The rockets went home for fuel. The jets went home for fuel. The helicopters hung on—still ready, still waiting.

The rockets came back and roared harmlessly about, and went away again. They stayed away. The helicopter men never faltered and never relaxed. The prison below them was washed with light—from the guard posts on the walls, from the cell blocks themselves, from the mobile lights of the guard squadrons surrounding the walls.

North of the prison, on the long, flat, damp developments of reclaimed land, the matchbox row houses of the clerical neighborhoods showed lights in every window as the figgers stood ready to repel invasion from their undesired neighbors to the east, the wipes. In the crowded tenements of the laborers' quarters, the wipes shouted from window to window; and there were crowds in the bright streets.

"The whole bloody thing's going to blow up!" a helicopter bombardier yelled bitterly to his pilot, above the flutter and roar of the whirling blades. "Look at the mobs in Greaserville! The first breakout from the Jug's going to start a fight like you never saw and we'll be right in the middle of it!"

MY LADY GREENSLEEVES

He was partly right. He would be right in the middle of it—for every man, woman and child in the city-state would be right in the middle of it. There was no place anywhere that would be spared. *No mixing.* That was the prescription that kept the city-state alive. There's no harm in a family fight—and aren't all mechanics a family, aren't all laborers a clan, aren't all clerks and office workers related by closer ties than blood or skin?

But the declassed cons of the Jug were the dregs of every class; and once they spread, the neat compartmentation of society was pierced. The breakout would mean riot on a bigger scale than any prison had ever known.

But he was also partly wrong. Because the breakout wasn't seeming to come.

*

The Jug itself was coming to a boil.

Honor Block A, relaxed and easy at the end of another day, found itself shaken alert by strange goings-on. First there was the whir and roar of the Air Force overhead. *Trouble.* Then there was the sudden arrival of extra guards, doubling the normal complement—day-shift guards, summoned away from their comfortable civil-service homes at some urgent call. *Trouble for sure.*

Honor Block A wasn't used to trouble. A Block was as far from the Greensleeves of O Block as you could get and still be in the Jug. Honor Block A belonged to the prison's halfbreeds—the honor prisoners, the trusties who did guards' work because there weren't enough guards to go around. They weren't Apaches or Piutes; they were camp-following Injuns who had sold out for the white man's firewater. The price of their service was privilege—many privileges.

Item: TV sets in every cell. Item: Hobby tools, to make gadgets for the visitor trade—the only way an inmate could earn an honest dollar. Item: In consequence, an exact knowledge of everything the outside world knew and put on its TV screens (including the grim, alarming reports of "trouble at Estates-General"), and the capacity to convert their "hobby tools" to—other uses.

An honor prisoner named Wilmer Lafon was watching the TV screen with an expression of rage and despair.

FREDERIK POHL

Lafon was a credit to the Jug—he was a showpiece for visitors. Prison rules provided for prisoner training—it was a matter of "rehabilitation." Prisoner rehabilitation is a joke and a centuries-old one at that; but it had its serious uses, and one of them was to keep the prisoners busy. It didn't much matter at what.

Lafon, for instance, was being "rehabilitated" by studying architecture. The guards made a point of bringing inspection delegations to his cell to show him off. There were his walls, covered with pin-ups—but not of women. The pictures were sketches Lafon had drawn himself; they were of buildings, highways, dams and bridges; they were splendidly conceived and immaculately executed.

*

"Looka that!" the guards would rumble to their guests. "There isn't an architect on the outside as good as this boy! What do you say, Wilmer? Tell the gentlemen—how long you been taking these correspondence courses in architecture? Six years! Ever since he came to the Jug."

And Lafon would grin and bob his head, and the delegation would go, with the guards saying something like: "Believe me, that Wilmer could design a whole skyscraper—and it wouldn't fall down, either!"

And they were perfectly, provably right. Not only could Inmate Lafon design a skyscraper, but he had already done so. More than a dozen of them. And none had fallen down.

Of course, that was more than six years back, before he was convicted and sent to the Jug. He would never design another. Or if he did, it would never be built. For the plain fact of the matter was that the Jug's rehabilitation courses were like rehabilitation in every prison since crime and punishment began. They kept the inmates busy. They made a show of purpose for an institution that had never had a purpose beyond punishment.

And that was all.

For punishment for a crime is not satisfied by a jail sentence. How does it hurt a man to feed and clothe and house him, with the bills paid by the state? Lafon's punishment was that he, as an architect, was *through*.

Savage tribes used to lop off a finger or an ear to punish a criminal. Civilized societies confine their amputations to bits and pieces of the personality. Chop-chop, and a man's reputation comes off; chop-chop

19

again, and his professional standing is gone; chop-chop, and he has lost the respect and trust of his fellows.

The jail itself isn't the punishment. The jail is only the shaman's hatchet that performs the amputation. If rehabilitation in a jail worked—if it were *meant* to work—it would be the end of jails.

Rehabilitation? Rehabilitation for what?

*

Wilmer Lafon switched off the television set and silently pounded his fist into the wall.

Never again to return to the Professional class! For, naturally, the conviction had cost him his membership in the Architectural Society and *that* had cost him his Professional standing.

But still—just to be out of the Jug, that would be something! And his whole hope of ever getting out lay not here in Honor Block A, but in the turmoil of the Greensleeves, a hundred meters and more than fifty armed guards away.

He was a furious man. He looked into the cell next door, where a con named Garcia was trying to concentrate on a game of Solitaire Splitfee. Once Garcia had been a Professional, too; he was the closest thing to a friend Wilmer Lafon had. Maybe he could now help to get Lafon where he wanted—*needed!*—to be.

Lafon swore silently and shook his head. Garcia was a spineless milksop, as bad as any clerk—Lafon was nearly sure there was a touch of the inkwell somewhere in his family. Shrewd and slippery enough, like all figgers. But you couldn't rely on him in a pinch.

Lafon would have to do it all himself.

He thought for a second, ignoring the rustle and mumble of the other honor prisoners of Block A. There was no help for it; he would have to dirty his hands with physical activity.

Outside on the deck, the guards were grumbling to each other. Lafon wiped the scowl off his black face, put on a smile, rehearsed what he was going to say, and politely rattled the door of his cell.

"Shut up down there!" one of the screws bawled. Lafon recognized the voice; it was the guard named Sodaro. That was all to the good. He knew Sodaro and he had some plans for him.

He rattled the cell door again and called: "Chief, can you come here a minute, please?"

Sodaro yelled: "Didn't you hear me? Shut up!" But he came wandering by and looked into Lafon's tidy little cell.

"What the devil do you want?" he growled.

Lafon said ingratiatingly: "What's going on, Chief?"

"Shut your mouth," Sodaro said absently and yawned. He hefted his shoulder holster comfortably. That O'Leary, what a production he had made of getting the guards back! And here he was, stuck in Block A on the night he had set aside for getting better acquainted with that little blue-eyed statistician from the Census office.

"Aw, Chief. The television says there's something going on in the Greensleeves. What's the score?"

Sodaro had no reason not to answer him, but it was his unvarying practice to make a con wait before doing anything the con wanted. He gave Lafon a ten-second stare before he relented.

"The score? Sauer and Flock took over Block O. What about it?"

Much, much about it! But Lafon looked away to hide the eagerness in his eyes. Perhaps, after all, it was not too late....

He suggested humbly: "You look a little sleepy. Do you want some coffee?"

"Coffee?" Sodaro scratched. "You got a cup for me?"

"Certainly! I've got one put aside—swiped it from the messhall—not the one I use myself."

"Um." Sodaro leaned on the cell door. "You know I could toss you in the Greensleeves for stealing from the messhall."

*

"Aw, chief!" Lafon grinned.

"You been looking for trouble. O'Leary says you were messing around with the bucks from the laundry detail," Sodaro said halfheartedly. But he didn't really like picking on Lafon, who was, after all, an agreeable inmate to have on occasion. "All right. Where's the coffee?"

They didn't bother with tanglefoot fields in Honor Block A. Sodaro just unlocked the door and walked in, hardly bothering to look at Lafon. He took three steps toward the neat little desk at the back of the cell, where

Lafon had rigged up a drawing board and a table, where Lafon kept his little store of luxury goods.

Three steps.

And then, suddenly aware that Lafon was very close to him, he turned, astonished—a little too late. He saw that Lafon had snatched up a metal chair; he saw Lafon swinging it, his black face maniacal; he saw the chair coming down.

He reached for his shoulder holster, but it was very much too late for that.

V

Captain O'Leary dragged the scared little wretch into the warden's office. He shook the con angrily. "Listen to this, Warden! The boys just brought this one in from the Shops Building. Do you know what he's been up to?"

The warden wheezed sadly and looked away. He had stopped even answering O'Leary by now. He had stopped talking to Sauer on the interphone when the big convict called, every few minutes, to rave and threaten and demand a doctor. He had almost stopped doing everything except worry and weep. But—still and all, he was the warden. He was the one who gave the orders.

O'Leary barked: "Warden, this little greaser has bollixed up the whole tangler circuit for the prison. If the cons get out into the yard now, you won't be able to tangle them. You know what that means? They'll have the freedom of the yard, and who knows what comes next?"

The warden frowned sympathetically. "Tsk, tsk."

O'Leary shook the con again. "Come on, Hiroko! Tell the warden what you told the guards."

The con shrank away from him. Sweat was glistening on his furrowed yellow forehead. "I—I had to do it, Cap'n! I shorted the wormcan in the tangler subgrid, but I had to! I got a signal—'Bollix the grid tonight or some day you'll be in the yard and we'll static you!' What could I do, Cap'n? I didn't want to—"

O'Leary pressed: "Who did the signal come from?"

The con only shook his head, perspiring still more.

The warden asked faintly: "What's he saying?"

22

FREDERIK POHL

O'Leary rolled his eyes to heaven. And this was the warden—couldn't even understand shoptalk from the mouths of his own inmates!

He translated: "He got orders from the prison underground to short-circuit the electronic units in the tangler circuit. They threatened to kill him if he didn't."

The warden drummed with his fingers on the desk.

"The tangler field, eh? My, yes. That is important. You'd better get it fixed, O'Leary. Right away."

"Fixed? Warden, who's going to fix it? You know as well as I do that every mechanic in the prison is a con. Even if one of the guards would do a thing like that—and I'd bust him myself if he did!—he wouldn't know where to start. That's mechanic work."

The warden swallowed. He had to admit that O'Leary was right. Naturally nobody but a mechanic—and a specialist electrician from a particular subgroup of the greaser class at that—could fix something like the tangler field generators.

He said absently: "Well, that's true enough. After all, 'Specialization is the goal of civilization,' you know."

O'Leary took a deep breath. He needed it.

He beckoned to the guard at the door. "Take this greaser out of here!"

The con shambled out, his head hanging.

*

O'Leary turned to the warden and spread his hands.

"Warden," he said, "don't you see how this thing is building up? Let's not just wait for the place to explode in our faces! Let me take a squad into Block O before it's too late."

The warden pursed his lips thoughtfully and cocked his head, as though he were trying to find some trace of merit in an unreasonable request.

He said at last: "No."

O'Leary made a passionate sound that was trying to be bad language, but he was too raging mad to articulate it. He walked stiffly away from the limp, silent warden and stared out the window.

At least, he told himself, *he* hadn't gone to pieces. It was his doing, not the warden's, that all the off-duty guards had been dragged double-time back to the prison, his doing that they were now ringed around the outer walls or scattered on extra-man patrols throughout the prison.

23

MY LADY GREENSLEEVES

It was something, but O'Leary couldn't believe that it was enough. He'd been in touch with half a dozen of the details inside the prison on the intercom and each of them had reported the same thing. In all of E-G, not a single prisoner was asleep. They were talking back and forth between the cells and the guards couldn't shut them up. They were listening to concealed radios and the guards didn't dare make a shakedown to find them. They were working themselves up to something. To what?

O'Leary didn't want ever to find out what. He wanted to go in there with a couple of the best guards he could get his hands on—shoot his way into the Greensleeves if he had to—and clean out the infection.

But the warden said no.

O'Leary stared balefully at the hovering helicopters.

The warden was the warden. He was placed in that position through the meticulously careful operations of the Civil Service machinery, maintained in that position year after year through the penetrating annual inquiries of the Reclassification Board. It was *subversive* to think that the Board could have made a mistake!

But O'Leary was absolutely sure that the warden was a scared, ineffectual jerk.

*

The interphone was ringing again. The warden picked up the handpiece and held it bonelessly at arm's length, his eyes fixed glassily on the wall. It was Sauer from the Greensleeves again. O'Leary could hear his maddened bray.

"I warned you, Warden!" O'Leary could see the big con's contorted face in miniature, in the view screen of the interphone. The grin was broad and jolly, the snake's eyes poisonously cold. "I'm going to give you five minutes, Warden, you hear? Five minutes! And if there isn't a medic in here in five minutes to take care of my boy Flock—your guards have had it! I'm going to slice off an ear and throw it out the window, you hear me? And five minutes later, another ear. And five minutes later—"

The warden groaned weakly. "I've called for the prison medic, Sauer. Honestly I have! I'm sure he's coming as rapidly as he—"

"Five minutes!" And the ferociously grinning face disappeared.

O'Leary leaned forward. "Warden, let me take a squad in there!"

24

The warden gazed at him for a blank moment "Squad? No, O'Leary. What's the use of a squad? It's a medic I have to get in there. I have a responsibility to those guards and if I don't get a medic—"

A cold, calm voice from the door: "I am here, Warden."

O'Leary and the warden both jumped up.

The medic nodded slightly. "You may sit down."

"Oh, Doctor! Thank heaven you're here!" The warden was falling all over himself, getting a chair for his guest, flustering about.

O'Leary said sharply: "Wait a minute, Warden. You can't let the doctor go in alone!"

"He isn't alone!" The doctor's intern came from behind him, scowling belligerently at O'Leary. Youngish, his beard pale and silky, he was a long way from his first practice. "I'm here to assist him!"

O'Leary put a strain on his patience. "They'll eat you up in there, Doc! Those are the worst cons in the prison. They've got two hostages already. What's the use of giving them two more?"

The medic fixed him with his eyes. He was a tall man and he wore his beard proudly. "Guard, do you think you can prevent me from healing a sufferer?" He folded his hands over his abdomen and turned to leave.

The intern stepped aside and bowed his head.

O'Leary surrendered. "All right, you can go. But I'm coming with you—with a squad!"

*

Inmate Sue-Ann Bradley cowered in her cell. The Greensleeves was jumping. She had never—no, *never*, she told herself wretchedly—thought that it would be anything like this. She listened unbelievingly to the noise the released prisoners were making, smashing the chairs and commodes in their cells, screaming threats at the bound guards.

She faced the thought with fear, and with the sorrow of a murdered belief that was worse than fear. It was bad that she was in danger of dying right here and now, but what was even worse was that the principles that had brought her to the Jug were dying, too.

Wipes were *not* the same as Civil-Service people!

A bull's roar from the corridor and a shocking crash of glass—that was Flock, and apparently he had smashed the TV interphone.

25

MY LADY GREENSLEEVES

"What in the world are they *doing?*" Inmate Bradley sobbed to herself. It was beyond comprehension. They were yelling words that made no sense to her, threatening punishments on the guards that she could barely imagine. Sauer and Flock were laborers; some of the other rioting cons were clerks, mechanics—even Civil-Service or Professionals, for all she could tell. But she could hardly understand any of them. Why was the quiet little Chinese clerk in Cell Six setting fire to his bed?

There did seem to be a pattern, of sorts. The laborers were rocketing about, breaking things at random. The mechanics were pleasurably sabotaging the electronic and plumbing installations. The white-collar categories were finding their dubious joys in less direct ways—liking setting fire to a bed. But what a mad pattern!

The more Sue-Ann saw of them, the less she understood.

It wasn't just that they *talked* differently. She had spent endless hours studying the various patois of shoptalk and it had defeated her; but it wasn't just that.

It was bad enough when she couldn't understand the words—as when that trusty Mathias had ordered her in wipe shoptalk to mop out her cell. But what was even worse was not understanding the thought behind the words.

Sue-Ann Bradley had consecrated her young life to the belief that all men were created free and equal—and alike. Or alike in all the things that mattered, anyhow. Alike in hopes, alike in motives, alike in virtues. She had turned her back on a decent Civil-Service family and a promising Civil-Service career to join the banned and despised Association for the Advancement of the Categoried Classes—

Screams from the corridor outside.

Sue-Ann leaped to the door of her cell to see Sauer clutching at one of the guards. The guard's hands were tied, but his feet were free; he broke loose from the clumsy clown with the serpent's eyes, almost fell, ran toward Sue-Ann.

There was nowhere else to run. The guard, moaning and gasping, tripped, slid, caught himself and stumbled into her cell. "Please!" he begged. "That crazy Sauer—he's going to cut my ear off! For heaven's sake, ma'am—stop him!"

*

Sue-Ann stared at him, between terror and tears. Stop Sauer! If only she could. The big redhead was lurching stiffly toward them—raging, but not so angry that the water-moccasin eyes showed heat.

"Come here, you figger scum!" he roared.

The epithet wasn't even close—the guard was Civil Service through and through—but it was like a reviving whip-sting to Sue-Ann Bradley.

"Watch your language, Mr. Sauer!" she snapped incongruously.

Sauer stopped dead and blinked.

"Don't you dare hurt him!" she warned. "Don't you see, Mr. Sauer, you're playing into their hands? They're trying to divide us. They pit mechanic against clerk, laborer against armed forces. And you're helping them! Brother Sauer, I beg—"

The redhead spat deliberately on the floor.

He licked his lips, and grinned an amiable clown's grin, and said in his cheerful, buffoon bray: "Auntie, go verb your adjective adjective noun."

Sue-Ann Bradley gasped and turned white. She had known such words existed—but only theoretically. She had never expected to *hear* them. And certainly she would never have believed she would hear them, applied to her, from the lips of a—a *laborer*.

At her knees, the guard shrieked and fell to the floor.

"Sauer! Sauer!" A panicky bellow from the corridor; the red-haired giant hesitated. "Sauer, come on out here! There's a million guards coming up the stairs. Looks like trouble!"

Sauer said hoarsely to the unconscious guard: "I'll take care of *you*." And he looked blankly at the girl, and shook his head, and hurried back outside to the corridor.

Guards were coming, all right—not a million of them, but half a dozen or more. And leading them all was the medic, calm, bearded face looking straight ahead, hands clasped before him, ready to heal the sick, comfort the aged or bring new life into the world.

"Hold it!" shrieked little Flock, crouched over the agonizing blister on his abdomen, gun in hand, peering insanely down the steps. "Hold it or—"

"Shut up." Sauer called softly to the approaching group: "Let only the doc come up. Nobody else!"

The intern faltered; the guards stopped dead; the medic said calmly: "I must have my intern with me." He glanced at the barred gate wonderingly.

27

Sauer hesitated. "Well—all right. But no guards!"

A few yards away, Sue-Ann Bradley was stuffing the syncoped form of the guard into her small washroom.

It was time to take a stand. No more cowering, she told herself desperately. No more waiting. She closed the door on the guard, still unconscious, and stood grimly before it. Him, at least, she would save if she could. They could get him, but only over her dead body.

Or anyway, she thought with a sudden throbbing in her throat, over her body.

*

VI

After O'Leary and the medic left, the warden tottered to a chair—but not for long. His secretary appeared, eyes bulging. "The governor!" he gasped.

Warden Schluckebier managed to say: "Why, Governor! How good of you to come—"

The governor shook him off and held the door open for the men who had come with him. There were reporters from all the news services, officials from the township governments within the city-state. There was an Air GI with major's leaves on his collar—"Liaison, sir," he explained crisply to the warden, "just in case you have any orders for our men up there." There were nearly a dozen others.

The warden was quite overcome.

The governor rapped out: "Warden, no criticism of you, of course, but I've come to take personal charge. I'm superseding you under Rule Twelve, Paragraph A, of the Uniform Civil Service Code. Right?"

"Oh, *right!*" cried the warden, incredulous with joy.

"The situation is bad—perhaps worse than you think. I'm seriously concerned about the hostages those men have in there. And I had a call from Senator Bradley a short time ago—"

"Senator Bradley?" echoed the warden.

"Senator *Sebastian* Bradley. One of our foremost civil servants," the governor said firmly. "It so happens that his daughter is in Block O as an inmate."

The warden closed his eyes. He tried to swallow, but the throat muscles were paralyzed.

"There is no question," the governor went on briskly, "about the propriety of her being there. She was duly convicted of a felonious act, namely conspiracy and incitement to riot. But you see the position."

The warden saw all too well.

"Therefore," said the governor. "I intend to go in to Block O myself. Sebastian Bradley is an old and personal friend—as well," he emphasized, "as being a senior member of the Reclassification Board. I understand a medic is going to Block O. I shall go with him."

The warden managed to sit up straight. "He's gone. I mean they already left, Governor. But I assure you Miss Brad—Inmate Bradley—that is, the young lady is in no danger. I have already taken precautions," he said, gaining confidence as he listened to himself talk. "I—uh—I was deciding on a course of action as you came in. See, Governor, the guards on the walls are all armed. All they have to do is fire a couple of rounds into the yard and then the 'copters could start dropping tear gas and light fragmentation bombs and—"

The governor was already at the door. "You will *not*," he said; and: "Now which way did they go?"

*

O'Leary was in the yard and he was smelling trouble, loud and strong. The first he knew that the rest of the prison had caught the riot fever was when the lights flared on in Cell Block A.

"That Sodaro!" he snarled, but there wasn't time to worry about that Sodaro. He grabbed the rest of his guard detail and double-timed it toward the New Building, leaving the medic and a couple of guards walking sedately toward the Old. Block A, on the New Building's lowest tier, was already coming to life; a dozen yards, and Blocks B and C lighted up.

And a dozen yards more and they could hear the yelling; and it wasn't more than a minute before the building doors opened.

The cons had taken over three more blocks. How? O'Leary didn't take time even to guess. The inmates were piling out into the yard. He took one look at the rushing mob. Crazy! It was Wilmer Lafon leading the rioters, with a guard's gun and a voice screaming threats! But O'Leary didn't take time to worry about an honor prisoner gone bad, either.

"Let's get out of here!" he bellowed to the detachment, and they ran.

Just plain ran. Cut and ran, scattering as they went.

29

MY LADY GREENSLEEVES

"Wait!" screamed O'Leary, but they weren't waiting. Cursing himself for letting them get out of hand, O'Leary salvaged two guards and headed on the run for the Old Building, huge and dark, all but the topmost lights of Block O.

They saw the medic and his escort disappearing into the bulk of the Old Building and they saw something else. There were inmates between them and the Old Building! The Shops Building lay between—with a dozen more cell blocks over the workshops that gave it its name—and there was a milling rush of activity around its entrance, next to the laundry shed—

The laundry shed.

O'Leary stood stock still. Lafon leading the breakout from Block A. The little greaser who was a trusty in the Shops Building sabotaging the yard's tangler circuit. Sauer and Flock taking over the Greensleeves with a manufactured knife and a lot of guts.

Did it fit together? Was it all part of a plan?

That was something to find out—but not just then. "Come on," O'Leary cried to the two guards, and they raced for the temporary safety of the main gates.

The whole prison was up and yelling now.

O'Leary could hear scattered shots from the beat guards on the wall—*Over their heads, over their heads!* he prayed silently. And there were other shots that seemed to come from inside the walls—guards shooting, or convicts with guards' guns, he couldn't tell which. The yard was full of convicts now, in bunches and clumps; but none near the gate. And they seemed to have lost some of their drive. They were milling around, lit by the searchlights from the wall, yelling and making a lot of noise ... but going nowhere in particular. Waiting for a leader, O'Leary thought, and wondered briefly what had become of Lafon.

"You Captain O'Leary?" somebody demanded.

*

He turned and blinked. Good Lord, the governor! He was coming through the gate, waving aside the gate guards, alone. "You him?" the governor repeated. "All right, glad I found you. I'm going into Block O with you."

O'Leary swallowed and waved inarticulately at the teeming cons. True, there were none immediately near by—but there were plenty in the yard!

30

Riots meant breaking things up; already the inmates had started to break up the machines in the laundry shed and the athletic equipment in the yard lockers. When they found a couple of choice breakables like O'Leary and the governor, they'd have a ball!

"But, Governor—"

"But my foot! Can you get me in there or can't you?"

O'Leary gauged their chances. It wasn't more than fifty feet to the main entrance to the Old Building—not at the moment guarded, since all the guards were in hiding or on the walls, and not as yet being invaded by the inmates at large.

He said: "You're the boss. Hold on a minute—" The searchlights were on the bare yard cobblestones in front of them; in a moment, the searchlights danced away.

"Come on!" cried O'Leary, and jumped for the entrance. The governor was with him and a pair of the guards came stumbling after.

They made it to the Old Building.

Inside the entrance, they could hear the noise from outside and the yelling of the inmates who were still in their cells. But around them was nothing but gray steel walls and the stairs going all the way up to Block O.

"Up!" panted O'Leary, and they clattered up the steel steps.

They would have made it—if it hadn't been for the honor inmate, Wilmer Lafon, who knew what he was after and had headed for the Greensleeves through the back way. In fact, they did make it—but not the way they planned. "Get out of the way!" yelled O'Leary at Lafon and the half-dozen inmates with him; and "Go to hell!" screamed Lafon, charging; and it was a rough-and-tumble fight, and O'Leary's party lost it, fair and square.

So when they got to Block O, it was with the governor marching before a convict-held gun, and with O'Leary cold unconscious, a lump from a gun-butt on the side of his head.

*

As they came up the stairs, Sauer was howling at the medic: "You got to fix up my boy! He's dying and all you do is sit there!"

The medic said patiently: "My son, I've dressed his wound. He is under sedation and I must rest. There will be other casualties."

MY LADY GREENSLEEVES

Sauer raged, but that was as far as it went. Even Sauer wouldn't attack a medic. He would as soon strike an Attorney, or even a Director of Funerals. It wasn't merely that they were Professionals. Even among the Professional class, they were special; not superior, exactly, but *apart*. They certainly were not for the likes of Sauer to fool with and Sauer knew it.

"Somebody's coming!" bawled one of the other freed inmates.

*

Sauer jumped to the head of the steps, saw that Lafon was leading the group, stepped back, saw whom Lafon's helpers were carrying and leaped forward again.

"Cap'n O'Leary!" he roared. "Gimme!"

"Shut up," said Wilmer Lafon, and pushed the big redhead out of the way. Sauer's jaw dropped and the snake eyes opened wide.

"Wilmer," he protested feebly. But that was all the protest he made, because the snake's eyes had seen that Lafon held a gun. He stood back, the big hands half outstretched toward the unconscious guard captain, O'Leary, and the cold eyes became thoughtful.

And then he saw who else was with the party. "Wilmer! You got the governor there!"

Lafon nodded. "Throw them in a cell," he ordered, and sat down on a guard's stool, breathing hard. It had been a fine fight on the steps, before he and his boys had subdued the governor and the guards, but Wilmer Lafon wasn't used to fighting. Even six years in the Jug hadn't turned an architect into a laborer; physical exertion simply was not his metier.

Sauer said coaxingly: "Wilmer, won't you leave me have O'Leary for a while? If it wasn't for me and Flock, you'd still be in A Block and—"

"Shut up," Lafon said again, gently enough, but he waved the gun muzzle. He drew a deep breath, glanced around him and grinned. "If it wasn't for you and Flock," he mimicked. "If it wasn't for you and Flock! Sauer, you wipe clown, do you think it took *brains* to file down a shiv and start things rolling? If it wasn't for *me*, you and Flock would have beaten up a few guards, and had your kicks for half an hour, and then the whole prison would fall in on you! It was me, Wilmer Lafon, who set things up and you know it!"

He was yelling and suddenly he realized he was yelling. And what was the use, he demanded of himself contemptuously, of trying to argue with

32

a bunch of lousy wipes and greasers? They'd never understand the long, soul-killing hours of planning and sweat. They wouldn't realize the importance of the careful timing—of arranging that the laundry cons would start a disturbance in the yard right after the Greensleeves hard-timers kicked off the riot, of getting the little greaser Hiroko to short-circuit the yard field so the laundry cons could start their disturbances.

It took a *Professional* to organize and plan—yes, and to make sure that he himself was out of it until everything was ripe, so that if anything went wrong, *he* was all right. It took somebody like Wilmer Lafon—a *Professional*, who had spent six years too long in the Jug—

And who would shortly be getting out.

VII

Any prison is a ticking bomb. Estates-General was in process of going off.

From the Greensleeves, where the trouble had started, clear out to the trusty farms that ringed the walls, every inmate was up and jumping. Some were still in their cells—the scared ones, the decrepit oldsters, the short-termers who didn't dare risk their early discharge. But for every man in his cell, a dozen were out and yelling.

A torch, licking as high as the hanging helicopters, blazing up from the yard—that was the laundry shed. Why burn the laundry? The cons couldn't have said. It was burnable and it was there—burn it!

The yard lay open to the wrath of the helicopters, but the helicopters made no move. The cobblestones were solidly covered with milling men. The guards were on the walls, sighting down their guns; the helicopter bombardiers had their fingers on the bomb trips. There had been a few rounds fired over the heads of the rioters, at first.

Nothing since.

In the milling mob, the figures clustered in groups. The inmates from Honor Block A huddled under the guards' guns at the angle of the wall. They had clubs—all the inmates had clubs—but they weren't using them.

Honor Block A: On the outside, Civil Service and Professionals. On the inside, the trusties, the "good" cons.

They weren't the type for clubs.

With all of the inmates, you looked at them and you wondered what twisted devil had got into their heads to land them in the Jug. Oh, perhaps you could understand it—a little bit, at least—in the case of the figgers in Blocks B and C, the greasers in the Shop Building—that sort. It was easy enough for some of the Categoried Classes to commit a crime and thereby land in jail.

Who could blame a wipe for trying to "pass" if he thought he could get away with it? But when he didn't get away with it, he wound up in the Jug and that was logical enough. And greasers liked Civil-Service women—everyone knew that.

There was almost a sort of logic to it, even if it was a sort of inevitable logic that made decent Civil-Service people see red. You *had* to enforce the laws against rape if, for instance, a greaser should ask an innocent young female postal clerk for a date. But you could understand what drove him to it. The Jug was full of criminals of that sort. And the Jug was the place for them.

But what about Honor Block A?

Why would a Wilmer Lafon—a certified public architect, a Professional by category—do his own car repairs and get himself jugged for malpractice? Why would a dental nurse sneak back into the laboratory at night and cast an upper plate for her mother? She must have realized she would be caught.

But she had done it. And she had been caught; and there she was, this wild night, huddled under the helicopters, uncertainly waving the handle of a floor mop. It was a club.

She shivered and turned to the stocky convict next to her. "Why don't they break down the gate?" she demanded. "How long are we going to hang around here, waiting for the guards to get organized and pick us all off one at a time?"

The convict next to her sighed and wiped his glasses with a beefy hand. Once he had been an Income-Tax Accountant, disbarred and convicted on three counts of impersonating an attorney when he took the liberty of making changes in a client's lease. He snorted: "They expect us to do *their* dirty work."

The two of them glared angrily and fearfully at the other convicts in the yard.

And the other convicts, huddled greaser with greaser, wipe with wipe, glared ragingly back. It wasn't *their* place to plan the strategy of a prison break.

*

Captain Liam O'Leary muttered groggily: "They don't want to escape. All they want is to make trouble. I know cons!"

He came fully awake and sat up and focused his eyes. His head was hammering.

That girl, that Bradley, was leaning over him. She looked scared and sick. "Sit still! Sauer is just plain crazy—listen to them yelling out there!"

O'Leary sat up and looked around, one hand holding his drumming skull.

"They *do* want to escape," said Sue-Ann Bradley. "Listen to what they're saying!"

*

O'Leary discovered that he was in a cell. There was a battle going on outside. Men were yelling, but he couldn't see them.

He jumped up, remembering. "The governor!"

Sue-Ann Bradley said: "He's all right. I *think* he is, anyway. He's in the cell right next to us, with a couple guards. I guess they came up with you." She shivered as the yells in the corridor rose. "Sauer is angry at the medic," she explained. "He wants him to fix Flock up so they can—'crush out,' I think he said. The medic says he can't do it. You see, Flock got burned pretty badly with a knife he made. Something about the tanglefoot field—"

"Eddy currents," said O'Leary dizzily.

"Anyway, the medic—"

"Never mind the medic. What's Lafon doing?"

"Lafon? The Negro?" Sue-Ann Bradley frowned. "I didn't know his name. He started the whole thing, the way it sounds. They're waiting for the mob down in the yard to break out and then they're going to make a break—"

"Wait a minute," growled O'Leary. His head was beginning to clear. "What about you? Are you in on this?"

She hung between laughter and tears. Finally: "Do I *look* as if I am?"

O'Leary took stock. Somehow, somewhere, the girl had got a length of metal pipe—from the plumbing, maybe. She was holding it in one hand, supporting him with the other. There were two other guards in the cell, both out cold—one from O'Leary's squad, the other, O'Leary guessed, a desk guard who had been on duty when the trouble started.

35

"I wouldn't let them in," she said wildly. "I told them they'd have to kill me before they could touch that guard."

O'Leary said suspiciously: "You belonged to that Double-A-C, didn't you? You were pretty anxious to get in the Greensleeves, disobeying Auntie Mathias's orders. Are you sure you didn't know this was going to—"

It was too much. She dropped the pipe, buried her head in her hands. He couldn't tell if she laughed or wept, but he could tell that it hadn't been like that at all.

"I'm sorry," he said awkwardly, and touched her helplessly on the shoulder.

*

He turned and looked out the little barred window, because he couldn't think of any additional way to apologize. He heard the wavering beat in the air and saw them—bobbing a hundred yards up, their wide metal vanes fluttering and hissing from the jets at the tips. The GI 'copters. Waiting—as everyone seemed to be waiting.

Sue-Ann Bradley asked shakily: "Is anything the matter?"

O'Leary turned away. It was astonishing, he thought, what a different perspective he had on those helicopter bombers from inside Block O. Once he had cursed the warden for not ordering at least tear gas to be dropped.

He said harshly: "Nothing. Just that the 'copters have the place surrounded."

"Does it make any difference?"

He shrugged. Does it make a difference? The difference between trouble and tragedy, or so it now seemed to Captain O'Leary. The riot was trouble. They could handle it, one way or another. It was his job, any guard's job, to handle *prison* trouble.

But to bring the GIs into it was to invite race riot. Not prison riot—race riot. Even the declassed scum in the Jug would fight back against the GIs. They were used to having the Civil-Service guards over them—that was what guards were for. Civil-Service guards guarded. What else? It was their job—as clerking was a rigger's job, and machines were a greaser's, and pick-and-shovel strong-arm work was a wipe's.

But the Armed Services—their job was to defend the country against forces outside—in a world that had only inside forces. The cons wouldn't hold still under attack from the GIs. *Race riot!*

36

But how could you tell that to a girl like this Bradley? O'Leary glanced at her covertly. She *looked* all right. Rather nice-looking, if anything. But he hadn't forgotten why she was in E-G. Joining a terrorist organization, the Association for the Advancement of the Categoried Classes.

Actually getting up on street corners and proposing that greasers' children be allowed to go to school with GIs, that wipes inter-marry with Civil Service. Good Lord, they'd be suggesting that doctors eat with laymen next!

The girl said evenly: "Don't look at me that way. I'm not a monster."

O'Leary coughed. "Sorry. I didn't know I was staring." She looked at him with cold eyes. "I mean," he said, "you don't *look* like anybody who'd get mixed up in—well, miscegenation."

"Miscegenation!" she blazed. "You're all alike! You talk about the mission of the Categoried Classes and the rightness of segregation, but it's always just the one thing that's in your minds—sex! I'll tell you this, Captain O'Leary—I'd rather many a decent, hard-working clerk any day than the sort of Civil-Service trash I've seen around here!"

O'Leary cringed. He couldn't help it. Funny, he told himself, I thought I was shockproof—but this goes too far!

A bull-roar from the corridor. Sauer.

O'Leary spun. The big redhead was yelling: "Bring the governor out here. Lafon wants to talk to him!"

*

O'Leary went to the door of the cell, fast.

A slim, pale con from Block A was pushing the governor down the hall, toward Sauer and Lafon. The governor was a strong man, but he didn't struggle. His face was as composed and remote as the medic's; if he was afraid, he concealed it extremely well.

Sue-Ann Bradley stood beside O'Leary. "What's happening?"

He kept his eyes on what was going on. "Lafon is going to try to use the governor as a shield, I think." The voice of Lafon was loud, but the noises outside made it hard to understand. But O'Leary could make out what the dark ex-Professional was saying: "—know damn well you did something. But what? *Why don't they crush out?*"

Mumble-mumble from the Governor. O'Leary couldn't hear the words.

MY LADY GREENSLEEVES

But he could see the effect of them in Lafon's face, hear the rage in Lafon's voice. "Don't call me a liar, you civvy punk! You did something. I had it all planned, do you hear me? The laundry boys were going to rush the gate, the Block A bunch would follow—and then I was going to breeze right through. But you loused it up somehow. You must've!"

His voice was rising to a scream. O'Leary, watching tautly from the cell, thought: He's going to break. He can't hold it in much longer.

"All *right*!" shouted Lafon, and even Sauer, looming behind him, looked alarmed. "It doesn't matter what you did. I've got you now and *you* are going to get me out of here. You hear? I've got this gun and the two of us are going to walk right out, through the gate, and if anybody tries to stop us—"

"Hey," said Sauer, waking up.

"—if anybody tries to stop us, you'll get a bullet right in—"

"*Hey!*" Sauer was roaring loud as Lafon himself now. "What's this talk about the *two* of you? You aren't going to leave me and Flock!"

"Shut up," Lafon said conversationally, without taking his eyes off the governor.

But Sauer, just then, was not the man to say "shut up" to, and especially he was not a man to take your eyes away from.

"That's torn it," O'Leary said aloud. The girl started to say something. But he was no longer there to hear.

It looked very much as though Sauer and Lafon were going to tangle. And when they did, it was the end of the line for the governor.

*

Captain O'Leary hurtled out of the sheltering cell and skidded down the corridor. Lafon's face was a hawk's face, gleaming with triumph. As he saw O'Leary coming toward him, the hawk sneer froze. He brought the gun up, but O'Leary was a fast man.

O'Leary leaped on the lithe black honor prisoner. Lafon screamed and clutched; and O'Leary's lunging weight drove him back against the wall. Lafon's arm smacked against the steel grating and the gun went flying. The two of them clinched and fell, gouging, to the floor.

Grabbing the advantage, O'Leary hammered the con's head against the deck, hard enough to split a skull. And perhaps it split Lafon's, because the dark face twitched and froth appeared at the lips; and the body slacked.

One down!

Now Sauer was charging. O'Leary wriggled sidewise and the big redhead blundered crashing into the steel grate. Sauer fell and O'Leary caught at him. He tried hammering the head as he swarmed on top of the huge clown. But Sauer only roared the louder. The bull body surged under O'Leary and then Sauer was on top and O'Leary wasn't breathing. Not at all.

Good-by, Sue-Ann, O'Leary said silently, without meaning to say anything of the kind; and even then he wondered why he was saying it.

O'Leary heard a gun explode beside his head.

Amazing, he thought, I'm breathing again! The choking hands were gone from his throat.

It took him a moment to realize that it was Sauer who had taken the bullet, not him. Sauer who now lay dead, not O'Leary. But he realized it when he rolled over, and looked up, and saw the girl with the gun still in her hand, staring at him and weeping.

He sat up. The two guards still able to walk were backing Sue-Ann Bradley up. The governor was looking proud as an eagle, pleased as a mother hen.

The Greensleeves was back in the hands of law and order.

The medic came toward O'Leary, hands folded. "My son," he said, "if your throat needs—"

O'Leary interrupted him. "I don't need a thing, Doc! I've got everything I want right now."

VIII

Inmate Sue-Ann Bradley cried: "They're coming! O'Leary, they're coming!"

The guards who had once been hostages clattered down the steps to meet the party. The cons from the Greensleeves were back in their cells. The medic, after finishing his chores on O'Leary himself, paced meditatively out into the wake of the riot, where there was plenty to keep him busy. A faintly guilty expression tinctured his carven face. Contrary to his oath to care for all humanity in anguish, he had not liked Lafon or Sauer.

The party of fresh guards appeared and efficiently began re-locking the cells of the Greensleeves.

"Excuse me, Cap'n," said one, taking Sue-Ann Bradley by the arm. "I'll just put this one back—"

"I'll take care of her," said Liam O'Leary. He looked at her sideways as he rubbed the bruises on his face.

The governor tapped him on the shoulder. "Come along," he said, looking so proud of himself, so pleased. "Let's go out in the yard for a breath of fresh air." He smiled contentedly at Sue-Ann Bradley. "You, too."

O'Leary protested instinctively: "But she's an inmate!"

"And I'm a governor. Come along."

They walked out into the yard. The air was fresh, all right. A handful of cons, double-guarded by sleepy and irritable men from the day shift, were hosing down the rubble on the cobblestones. The yard was a mess, but it was quiet now. The helicopters were still riding their picket line, glowing softly in the early light that promised sunrise.

"My car," the governor said quietly to a state policeman who appeared from nowhere. The trooper snapped a salute and trotted away.

"I killed a man," said Sue-Ann Bradley, looking a little ill.

"You saved a man," corrected the governor. "Don't weep for that Lafon. He was willing to kill a thousand men if he had to, to break out of here."

"But he never did break out," said Sue-Ann.

The governor stretched contentedly. "He never had a chance. Laborers and clerks join together in a breakout? It would never happen. They don't even speak the same language—as you have discovered, my dear."

*

Sue-Ann blazed: "I still believe in the equality of Man!"

"Oh, please do," the governor said, straight-faced. "There's nothing wrong with that. Your father and I are perfectly willing to admit that men are equal—but we can't admit that all men are the *same*. Use your eyes! What you believe in is your business, but," he added, "when your beliefs extend to setting fire to segregated public lavatories as a protest move, which is what got you arrested, you apparently need to be taught a lesson. Well, perhaps you've learned it. You were a help here tonight and that counts for a lot."

Captain O'Leary said, face furrowed: "What about the warden, Governor? They say the category system is what makes the world go round;

40

it fits the right man to the right job and keeps him there. But look at Warden Schluckebier! He fell completely apart at the seams. He—"

"Turn that statement around, O'Leary."

"Turn—?"

The governor nodded. "You've got it reversed. Not the right man for the job—the right job for the man! We've got Schluckebier on our hands, see? He's been born; it's too late to do anything about that. He will go to pieces in an emergency. So where do we put him?"

O'Leary stubbornly clamped his jaw, frowning.

"We put him," the governor went on gently, "where the best thing to *do* in a crisis is to go to pieces! Why, O'Leary, you get some hot-headed man of action in here, and every time an inmate sneezes, you'll have bloodshed! And there's no harm in a prison riot. Let the poor devils work off steam. I wouldn't have bothered to get out of bed for it—except I was worried about the hostages. So I came down to make sure they were protected in the best possible way."

O'Leary's jaw dropped. "But you were—"

The governor nodded. "I was a hostage myself. That's one way to protect them, isn't it? By giving the cons a hostage that's worth more to them."

He yawned and looked around for his car. "So the world keeps going around," he said. "Everybody is somebody else's outgroup and maybe it's a bad thing, but did you ever stop to realize that we don't have wars any more? The categories stick tightly together. Who is to say that that's a bad thing?"

He grinned. "Reminds me of a story, if you two will pay attention to me long enough to listen. There was a meeting—this is an old, *old* story—a neighborhood meeting of the leaders of the two biggest women's groups on the block. There were eighteen Irish ladies from the Church Auxiliary and three Jewish ladies from B'nai B'rith. The first thing they did was have an election for a temporary chairwoman. Twenty-one votes were cast. Mrs. Grossinger from B'nai B'rith got three and Mrs. O'Flaherty from the Auxiliary got eighteen. So when Mrs. Murphy came up to congratulate Mrs. O'Flaherty after the election, she whispered: 'Good for you! But isn't it terrible, the way these Jews stick together?'"

He stood up and waved a signal as his long official car came poking hesitantly through the gate.

"Well," he declared professionally, "that's that. As we politicians say, any questions?"

Sue-Ann hesitated. "Yes, I guess I do have a question," she said. "What's a Jew?"

*

It was full dawn at last. The recall signal had come and the helicopters were swooping home to Hap Arnold Field.

A bombardier named Novak, red-eyed and grumpy, was amusing himself on the homeward flight by taking practice sights on the stream of work-bound mechanics as they fluttered over Greaserville.

"Could pick 'em off like pigeons," he said sourly to his pilot, as he dropped an imaginary bomb on a cluster of a dozen men. "For two cents, I'd do it, too. The only good greaser is a dead greaser."

His pilot, just as weary, said loftily: "Leave them alone. The best way to handle them is to leave them alone."

And the pilot was perfectly right; and that was the way the world went round, spinning slowly and unstoppably toward the dawn.

www.ingramcontent.com/pod-product-compliance
Lightning Source LLC
Chambersburg PA
CBHW020144150626
46552CB00021B/1611